Silly Miss Lilly

Fulton Books, Inc.
Meadville, PA

Published by Fulton Books 2021

ISBN 978-1-63710-139-1 (paperback)
ISBN 978-1-63710-140-7 (digital)

Printed in the United States of America

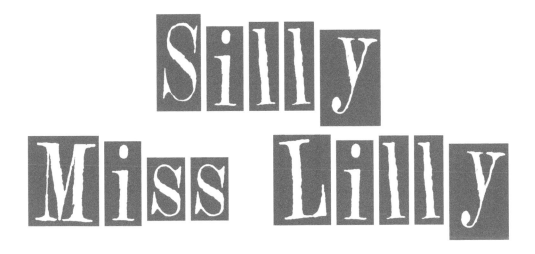

Silly Miss Lilly

Gretchen Dee Folsom

I want to share with you a great adventure I had with the lady who lives across the street.

I call her Silly Miss Lilly.

She is very thin and has hair that stands out on end.

She has feet like skis and always wears bright colors, sparkles, and crazy hats. Even her earrings match.

She comes out in the morning at about nine o'clock, gets on the bus, and off she goes.

I wonder where Silly Miss Lilly goes.

She comes back in the evening around four o'clock with different bags from different shops.

What does Silly Miss Lilly do with all those things?

*   *   *   *   *

One morning, I needed to find out where Silly Miss Lilly goes. That morning was rainy and very cold. I thought for sure she would not show, but out she came with a sparkle slicker and a hat to match. She even had raindrop earrings. Everything matched. We got on the bus, and she gave me a wink. I stopped for a moment. I didn't know what to think.

"Hello, I am Miss Lilly. You look like the girl who lives across the street."

I smiled and just sank into my seat.

*   *   *   *   *

Harriet's Emporium

BIG
SALE

OPEN

We rode for a while, and then Silly Miss Lilly gave out a yell. "Stop the bus! This store is having a big sale." She jumped off the bus with those feet like skis; she was so much faster than me. We entered the store, and she began to sing. I guess sales were Silly Miss Lilly's thing. She amazed me how fast she moved; she looked like a person who had something important to do. Out we came, and of course, she had bags in hand. She whistled to the bus driver to give her a hand. She gave him a big smile and a special wink and then settled right down next to my seat. What should I do? What should I say? I know I should have stayed home today.

*　*　*　*　*

"What is your name, little girl who lives across the street?"

"Della Rae," I said with a voice oh so meek.

"Lovely name. It has style," she said and then gave me a big smile.

* * * * *

We rode for a while, and all of a sudden my stomach gave out a growl. Then Silly Miss Lilly gave me a smile. "My dear," she said with a voice oh so sweet, "you need to get something to eat. There is a purpose that we both need to meet. We cannot shop and not eat. We need food to help us think."

* * * * *

ETHEL'S BAKERY

DANISH
on
SALE!

We rode by a bakery, and Silly Miss Lilly gave out a yell. "This place has the best Danish, and today they are on sale!"

The bus driver stopped, and out she ran with her sparkle purse in hand. "I will only take a minute. Would you like to give me a hand?"

"I guess so," I said, but I really didn't understand.

Then as fast as she moved, out we came with treats in hand. The whole bus gave us a hand.

She said to the bus driver, "We need to make a special stop. You know the one, the Silly Gift Shop." Silly Miss Lilly pulled at my sleeve. "This shop is just what you need. Some color, sparkles, a little bit of this, and a little of that. It is as simple as that."

* * * * *

We stopped at the shop that was purple and orange with a big green eye in the middle of the door. A sign was hanging from a long skinny nose. The sign read, "Everything Is on Sale. Just Follow Your Nose."

SILLY GIFT SHOP

SALE

Everything is
on SALE,
just follow your
nose

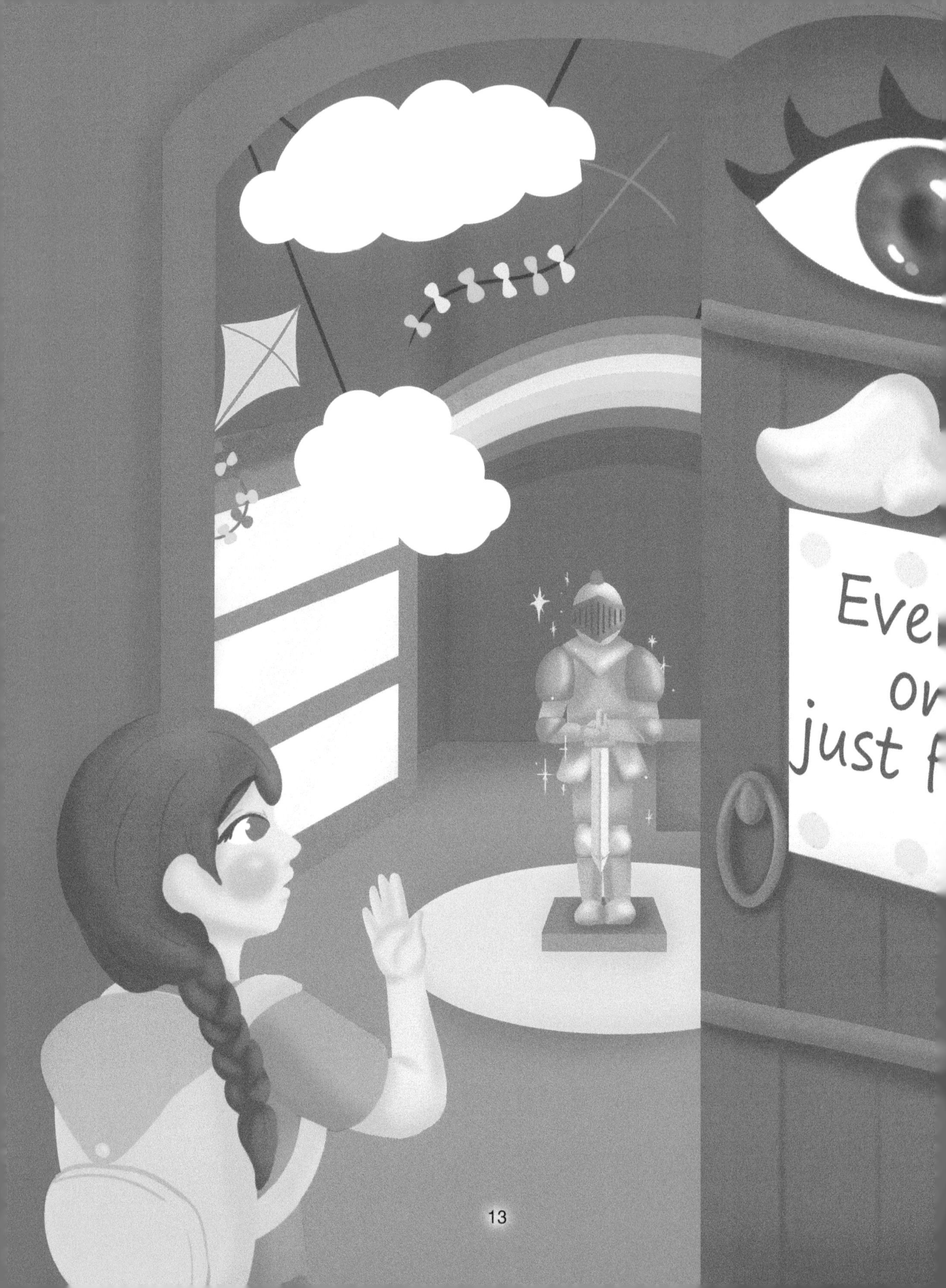
Eve
just f

Silly Miss Lilly said, "Just open the door. This is the place I think you will love to explore."

I opened the door, afraid of what I might see. What I saw was so amazing. I saw sparkling rainbows and kites that can fly at night. They even had a knight so shiny and bright that when you tickled his belly, he said, "Good night." There was so much to see.

Then Silly Miss Lilly said, "We have to leave by three".

*   *   *   *   *

"Enjoy, my dear. Look and explore. Just remember, we leave by three. I need to be home by four."

I explored all the different floors. One floor had just funny doors. My favorite was Mr. Blue who couldn't open because he had the flu and he was always blue. There was too much to see, and she wanted us to leave by three. Then all of a sudden, I heard that voice so sparkling and so very clear. "Della Rae, it's three. It's time for us to leave."

Why did we need to leave by three and be home by four? There was so much more to explore.

* * * * *

The bus horn was blowing, and the driver gave us all a yell. "This bus leaves at three! All aboard. We all need to be home by four!"

* * * * *

With her feet like skis and bags in hand, she took my hand, and to the bus we ran. We got on the bus with little or no fuss. We sat on our seats. She turned to me and gave me a smile.

All of a sudden the bus was dropping us at our stop. All the people on the bus smiled and waved, saying, "Hope to see you another day." We stood at the bus stop for a minute or so. I paused then asked, "What do you do with all those things, and why be home by four?"

She smiled and said, "I buy for the sick and the poor. I hope to put a smile on their faces and so much more. Why be home by four? Discount City Shopping Channel starts at four, and it shows me all the shops I need to explore."

She waved good-bye and gave me her smile.

I took a deep breath and a big sigh.

She's not Silly Miss Lilly to me anymore. She is Sweet Miss Lilly for evermore.

ABOUT THE AUTHOR

Gretchen Folsom has always dreamed of writing a children's book. With *Silly Miss Lilly*, her dream has come true.

Gretchen grew up in the Beacon Hill area of Seattle, Washington. Her maiden name is Caso, and most of her old friends from school still consider her a Caso. She went to both Catholic and public schools and graduated from Franklin High of Seattle.

Gretchen and her husband have lived in Washington, California, and Colorado; and they finally returned to Washington for good. She has two grown daughters and four grandchildren who are the love of her life.

Gretchen is a retired travel consultant of twenty-three years which, in turn, gives her more time to write.

She and her husband live in Auburn, Washington, on the Green River, which is about thirty miles south of Seattle. They enjoy watching the eagles and ducks.

Lightning Source UK Ltd.
Milton Keynes UK
UKHW051956250222
399240UK00003B/50